CRUEL KISS

CRUEL KISS

A CRUEL NOVELLA

K.A. LINDE

ISBN-13: 978-1948427654

1

WHITLEY

"I'm going to miss you."

I closed my eyes on a sigh as I stared out across the Manhattan skyline. Robert stood somewhere on the other side of his enormous penthouse, watching me. He'd been doing a lot of that over the last ten days. After he told me that he wasn't going on our planned holiday vacation and I'd have to spend the next two weeks on a private island without him.

He thought I was upset.

And I was.

Just ... not at him.

I was mad that I *wasn't* upset. I should have been. We'd been dating long enough that I should have felt *something* when he told me he couldn't get the time off work. I should have felt something at all about him even. But I didn't.

Robert Dawson was classic Upper East Side good looks with tailored suits, a European haircut, and a boarding school pedigree. He hosted Gatsby-level parties, and he was in love with me. Like *so* in love with me. All of that combined should have been enough for me to fall in love with him too ... right?

"Whit," Robert said. He stepped up to the window and leaned against the glass. He had on a navy-blue pin-striped suit and a furrow formed between his brows. "Talk to me."

"What is there to say?"

"You're mad that I'm not going."

"No," I whispered.

He sighed. "I did try to get the time off."

"It's fine."

"You've been off since I told you. It's not fine."

I shrugged and searched for my classic Whitley bravado. To all of my friends, I was the bubbly, flirtatious pixie, who always had a comeback and a wild dating story. But right now, I felt resigned to another relationship that wasn't working out. One that I'd thought might actually happen.

Robert grabbed my arm and spun me to look at him. There was fire in his eyes now. He held in everything he felt so succinctly that I rarely ever saw fire from him. It was a nice change.

"You can talk to me."

"I know."

"Is this because all of our friends are coupled up? You can hang out with Gavin and—"

"No," I said sharply. I didn't want to talk about Gavin King. "No, it's not that."

Robert slid his hands into his suit pockets. "Then, what? Because I've apologized a thousand times for this. I don't know how much more groveling you want from me. I've been perfectly accommodating with everything you've wanted out of this relationship. Relationships aren't normal for you, but it's been a learning curve for me too. So, if you have something to say, just spit it out."

I finally met his gaze and arched an eyebrow. Well, that was new and different. Robert had always been a nice guy. I hadn't expected him to push me here.

If he wanted the truth, then I owed him the truth.

"We should break up."

His jaw set as he froze to stone. "What?"

"I don't want to do this anymore."

He pushed away from the window. He didn't plead with me. I'd definitely thought that he would beg. Instead, he looked ready to rip his apartment apart. He picked up a glass and threw it against the wall. I jumped as it shattered into a million pieces.

"Robert!"

"All because I can't go on this trip?"

"No," I gasped.

"I thought our relationship was going great. I've

done everything you asked, Whitley. I ... I fell in love with you. This is self-sabotaging. You're running at the first sign of feelings."

"That's not true."

"Then, what is it? Because from where I'm standing, you look scared out of your mind that you feel anything at all. When we first got together, I understood that you were a perpetual flirt and believed you were this broken girlfriend. You have a fraught history with relationships, but it doesn't have to be this way."

All of that was true. Except how I felt about him. Because if anything, I felt numb, empty. The first time he'd ever pushed me about anything was this moment. It was too little, too late.

"Thank you for psychoanalyzing me," I quipped.

"Don't do that. Don't belittle this situation."

"You're the one who has it all figured out," I shot back. "Did you ever think that it's maybe just because I don't feel the same?"

"No, you're running scared, like normal."

"I don't love you," I whispered, the wind dropping out of my sails.

He staggered back a step but said nothing.

I shook my head with a sigh. I didn't feel anything at all. I wanted to. It would make a lot more sense if I did feel something for him. But it wasn't there, and no matter how much I tried, I couldn't make myself love someone that I didn't. If that made me flighty and a broken girlfriend, then fine. Paint me as the villain.

"I'm sorry."

"Don't go like this," he pleaded.

"I'm sorry," I repeated.

Then, I grabbed my suitcase, purse, and winter jacket and exited his apartment. I leaned my back against the door when it shut behind me. My stomach twisted in knots as I heard something shatter on the other side. Fuck.

Well, that couldn't have gone worse.

Not even a little bit.

I hadn't known that I was going to break up with him when I woke up this morning, but here I was. I took a fortifying breath and then released it. As much as it sucked to hurt him, I couldn't keep on like this. It was better to just yank the Band-Aid off.

I stepped onto the elevator as my phone dinged. I checked the message, expecting something from Robert, but it was my bestie, Anna English.

We're here! Come downstairs, bitch!

I closed my eyes and said a silent good-bye to Robert.

On to bigger and better.

Then, the elevator doors opened, and as I stomped

out, my foot caught on the exit, and I fell face-first into none other than Gavin King.

"Fuck!" I cried out.

There was nothing I could do in this situation. I was fucked. I was going to fall on the floor all because I hadn't been paying attention. And Gavin was going to be there to witness me looking like an idiot.

"Jesus," Gavin said as he reached for me.

Then, Gavin's arms came around my waist. I released a gasp as he pivoted sideways, twisting me in his arms. My caramel-colored hair dangled toward the floor. My hazel eyes went wide. The suitcase I'd been holding crashed against the lobby wall.

"I got you," he told me.

Heat flooded my system. I was a tiny thing, only about five feet tall, and Gavin was somewhere in the mid-six feet range. I felt like a rag doll in his arms. Normally, my personality made up for the extra inches I'd clearly lost in my adolescence, but right now, I had never been so glad to be this small.

Gavin was in jeans and a soft green sweater. His burnished dark auburn hair was carefully tousled, and a strand fell forward toward my face. His lips were mere inches away, and a secret dimple peeked out on one side. I was a goner for dimples.

Something crossed his face that I couldn't quite place. Desire? No, that was my imagination. Gavin wasn't into me. He had never been into me. We were friends. We'd played each other's wingman more than one time in the past. I was the flirt, and he was the player. We were too similar in so many ways. And neither of us was inclined to settle down. Then, I'd started dating one of his best friends, and he'd pulled farther and farther away.

Now, he was right here.

"Little clumsy, Bowen," he said, hastily putting me back on my feet.

We were still so close together. Not quite flush, but I could feel the heat off of him. I tilted my head back to look up at him. Again, something flashed in those emerald eyes.

He stepped backward and then went for my suitcase. "What happened?"

I cleared my throat. "I don't fucking know. Just tripped on something."

He flashed me a characteristic teasing smile. That was more the Gavin that I knew. "Where's Robert?"

"Oh," I said, fighting for carefree Whitley. "He's not coming."

Gavin arched an eyebrow. "Do I need to go upstairs and tell his ass to get moving?"

"He has to work."

"So? That's not an excuse."

I shrugged and met his gaze again.

"We broke up."

2

GAVIN

We broke up.

I heard the words that Whitley had said, but somehow, I couldn't comprehend them. Robert was one of my best friends. Before he'd gone for Whit, he'd asked if I was cool with it. The guys thought I had a thing for her even though we said time and time again that we were just friends. Of course, my friends were right. No matter how I denied it, I had this pull to Whit.

There was no one else in the world like this wild, flirtatious girl.

Which was why I had stayed far away. I burned all relationships that I touched. And Whit deserved better. So, I'd told Robert to go for it and regretted every minute I had to see them together.

But I was loyal to my boy.

"That sucks," I told her.

She shrugged. "It's not that surprising though, is it?"

It was surprising, only because I knew how much Robert was into her. I'd known him a long time and never known him to go after anyone like Whitley. She was driven, one of the leading plastic surgeons in Manhattan. Not to mention, funny and a party girl and over the top. The girls Robert liked were one of two extremes: serious, studious types or girls who ended up in rehab.

"He was really into you."

"Yeah," she muttered with a sad shrug. "That makes one of us."

And there it was. I'd spent so long focusing on how much Robert liked her that I'd forced myself not to pay attention to Whitley too closely. In my mind, she was incandescent and vibrant. A shooting star in the night. A bonfire on the beach. The rush of that first roller coaster drop.

But when I looked at her now—*really* looked at her for the first time in weeks—I saw something else. Her light had dimmed. Her smile didn't quite meet those sparkling eyes. She drooped. And now that I saw it, I couldn't unsee it.

"I know he's your friend," she said quickly, "but—"

"You don't have to explain yourself to me," I told her, sliding my hands into the pockets of my black peacoat. I'd ditched a suit for dark wash jeans and a green cashmere sweater. "If you're not happy, then you have to do what's best for you."

She brightened at those words, as if she hadn't expected them from me. Like she had been waiting for everyone to tell her to get back together with someone who didn't make her ridiculously happy.

"Thanks," she said as she pulled her own jacket on. "I guess that means it's you and me as the lone single friends."

I went hard on the dimples. "I guess it does."

She fluttered her eyelashes. "Wingman?"

"As long as you give me the good ones."

"Ha!" She rolled her eyes. "You can have the guys. I'll take the girls. I'm over men."

"You say that every time a relationship ends. Weren't you just lamenting that you were tired of women because they were so complicated?"

She shrugged. "Yeah, but I do like to eat out."

I winked at her. "Me too."

She pointed a finger toward my face. "Don't steal all the good ones from me, King."

"Hey," I said, holding my hands up. "I can't guarantee a thing. I'm irresistible."

She rolled her eyes dramatically, which was what I'd been hoping for. "A little sure of yourself, huh?"

"I have every reason to be."

Her eyes slid down my body, and for a split second, I was certain we were thinking the exact same thing.

Finally, she shrugged and said, "True."

I was saved from coming up with an adequately flirtatious response by English storming into the lobby of the building. Her hands were out, blonde hair flying.

"What the hell, Gavin? I sent you inside to make things faster, not to hold up the entire operation." She gestured to her Rolex. "We're on a schedule."

Whitley and I exchanged a look. English was a publicist by trade and one of the best in the business at that. She knew how to sass even the most famous among us. She had no qualms about doing it to her friends.

"Sorry. Whit tripped."

Whitley shrugged and hoisted her purse up her shoulder. "I'm ready now."

"Then, let's go," English said. She slung an arm around Whit, and they walked out into the wintry New York City mix.

It had snowed the night before. So, a soft white powder covered everything, except the streets and sidewalks, which were more like a black sludge. Ah, the joys of New York. A far cry from where I'd grown up in Midland, Texas. I'd been here long enough to love the city like home, but sometimes, I missed my family, the Texas weather, and fields of oil rigs.

Which I admitted was a strange thing to miss. But

when you grew up as an heir to the Texas oil fortune Dorset & King, it was somehow normal. My cousins ran the place back home, but I was the head of the New York division. Which meant I didn't handle day-to-day operations in the field, but rather worked with investors, business execs, and refineries in the northeast. Someone had to do it, and with my Harvard contacts, I'd been the prime choice.

A limo awaited us on the curb of Robert's building. English hopped inside, and Whitley followed after depositing her bag. I slid inside and took the spot next to English's boyfriend, Court Kensington. I'd gone to Harvard with Court and his best friend, Camden Percy. Camden would be joining us in Puerto Rico after Christmas with his wife, the infamous Katherine Van Pelt.

"About time," Court said.

I grinned. "What can I say? I make women swoon."

Whit snorted. "Hardly."

Larkin St. Vincent rolled her eyes at the lot of us. She was the reason we were going to this brand-new St. Vincent's Resort for the holidays. "Let's get moving."

Her boyfriend, Sam, slid his arm around her shoulders and grinned. "Where's Robert?"

"Didn't I tell you?" Lark asked. "He has to work."

"Oh, sorry, Whit," Sam said in his slight Southern drawl.

Whitley shifted uncomfortably.

English zeroed in on her fidgeting. "What happened?"

"Well, we broke up."

"What?" English gasped.

Lark's eyes widened. She threw her long red ponytail over her shoulder. "Oh my god, when?"

"Like ... just now."

I leaned back in my seat and tried to look conciliatory. But when Sam and Court both turned their attention to me at the same time, I could barely hold back my affronted look back at them.

"What?" I hissed at Court while Whitley was distracted, explaining her breakup to English and Lark.

Court smirked. "You know what."

I opened my mouth to object and then closed it. He was right. Fuck. My friends knew me too well sometimes.

Sam glanced at his girlfriend and back, as if checking to see that she wasn't paying attention. "Finally?"

"Hey, I'm not a dick," I grumbled.

Court held his fist out, and I thumped mine with his. "Oh, you're going to have a fun vacation."

The girls turned back to us at that.

English narrowed her eyes at Court. "What are you talking about?"

He pulled her in close. "Nothing, honey."

Court winked at me. I could barely suppress a smug look. My friends were assholes. I had been loyal to Robert about Whit since the start. I shouldn't move in on her when she was in rebound mode. But, damn ... hadn't I waited long enough?

3

WHITLEY

I'd never get used to taking a private jet. Let alone to the most exclusive resort in Puerto Rico that my friend's family *owned*.

I'd been born and raised in Dallas, Texas, by parents who wanted nothing more than for me to succeed when all they'd feared was that I'd end up in prison. I might have been a little wild in my youth. Of course, they'd all but disowned me when they found out that not only was I a bi girl, but I was—gasp— going into plastic surgery as well. Yes, plastic surgery was nearly as bad as bringing home my first girlfriend.

But either way, I hadn't grown up with the money of these Upper East Siders. I'd lucked into this friend group, and I never took them for granted. I was living my best life. Or at least, I was determined to continue to do so despite the two dozen sad text messages from Robert when I landed on the island.

"Wow," Lark said, glancing at my phone as it went off, one after the other after the other. "What's that?"

I shot her a look. "Robert."

"Eesh," English said. "Are you sure you want to break up with him?"

"I'm sure," I said as I reached for the bag.

"Okay." English held her hands up.

"Well, let's get to our private villas," Lark said. "That should help."

"Definitely," I agreed.

We pulled up in front of St. Vincent's Resort, and my jaw hit the ground. It was a sprawling complex of structures surrounding eight Olympic-sized pools. It looked like a total dream. A manager with sunbaked brown skin and floppy brown hair waited for us when we stepped out of the car.

"Hello, and welcome to St. Vincent's Resort: Puerto Rico. I am Paulo, your personal guide for the remainder of your stay. Should you need anything, I will assist you."

"Nice to meet you," Lark said.

"Larkin St. Vincent," Paulo said. "It is an honor to make your acquaintance."

She nodded at him. "We're delighted to be here."

Paulo had staff take care of the luggage and then sent the couples off with other personal guides.

"Whitley Bowen and Robert Dawson?" Paulo asked when Gavin and I were the only ones left.

"Oh, no," I said with a laugh. "Robert couldn't make it."

"Gavin King," he said, holding his hand out.

"Ah, I see. My apologies. I have you in separate villas. Would you prefer to be together?"

Gavin's eyes slid to mine. A question in them. Was he actually asking me if I'd prefer to stay in a villa with him?

A strangled laugh escaped my lips. "Aren't you going to have so much action that you'll want your own place?"

He chuckled. "Something like that."

"Separate then," Paulo said, making a note on an iPad. "This way."

He directed us down a cobbled path toward the villas. I was glad that I'd changed out of my winter clothes and into a sundress on the flight. It was eighty degrees and sunny. A perfect, beautiful day.

"This one is yours, Ms. Bowen," Paulo said, gesturing to a villa. "And this one is yours."

I glanced over and saw that Gavin King was right next door. We were a short distance from the rest of the villas. As if we'd been secluded together. I gulped.

"Thank you, Paulo."

I was on the patio, looking in on the giant suite before I realized Gavin still stood with Paulo.

He slipped him cash. "Thank you."

"Of course. Let me know if I can be of assistance."

As Paulo walked off, I bit my lip. "Should I have tipped him?"

"Don't worry about it. I got it." He hopped onto my patio and peered inside. "Your place is nice."

"I feel like an interloper."

Gavin laughed. "No way, Whit. You belong here. With us."

My phone dinged, and I rolled my eyes. Robert again. Man, I was going to have to block his number. I'd made my decision and flown out of the country without him.

Gavin took a step backward at the sound though. "I'll go check out my place. Meet you at the bar?"

"Sure," I said, meeting his gaze.

I sighed as Gavin walked out of the villa and left me all alone in this big room. No amount of excitement over the huge king-size bed, eighty-inch TV, hot tub, waterfall shower, or freestanding bathtub could make up for how empty it was.

I shook off the post-relationship blues and changed into my brightest bikini. It was the sunniest yellow in existence, and just having it on my body brightened my mood. When I got to the poolside bar, I ordered a piña colada, snagging a cabana just as my friends arrived. Lark and English dropped onto chairs on either side of me. As soon as servers saw Lark, she was bombarded with offers. There was a perk to being the daughter of the owners.

Once we all had drinks, they turned their eyes on me.

"So," English said.

"So," I repeated.

"Robert?" Lark asked.

I laughed and brushed it off, as I did everything else. "It was a long time coming and really for the better. He couldn't come. I wasn't feeling it anymore. Why not have fun while I'm here instead of moping around?"

"That'd be fine if any of that were true," English said pointedly.

"Ten days ago, Robert told me he wasn't coming, and I felt nothing." I took a sip of my drink. "I wanted to feel something, but I didn't. What I felt was almost relief."

Lark sighed. "Really? I thought you were so good together."

"He was *so* into me," I agreed. "I wanted to want someone like that."

"But you didn't?" English asked.

"I didn't. Like, isn't everyone obsessed with me?" I said on a laugh.

Lark rolled her eyes. "You're so ridiculous. At least you didn't do anything dramatic to him on your way out."

"Ceiling fan guy," English said.

I grinned wickedly. I'd found out some douche I was dating was cheating on me. So, like a sensible person, I turned off all his ceiling fans in the heat of the summer, put glitter on them, and left. What I wouldn't have given to see his face when he came home and turned those fans on. Glitter: the herpes of craft supplies.

"He didn't deserve any sabotage. He's a nice guy. I want him to find someone who is utterly head over heels for him like he was for me."

"And what do you want for you?" English asked.

"She wants to get laid," Lark said intuitively with a laugh.

I shrugged. She wasn't wrong. "I wouldn't say no."

"Are we talking rebound or vacation fling or ..."

"Fling," I said at once. "Rebound sounds icky. Like I'm here to hurt someone else. When, really, I just want us both to have some fun. Doesn't have to have any feelings, you know?"

"No," English and Lark said at once.

"Oh, shut up," I said as I sauntered into the pool. "You two both have the love of your life or whatever. You don't count."

"And you don't want that too?" Lark asked softly.

"Well, I'm not going to find it on vacation."

That was when the guys showed up. All three of our boys were fine as fuck. But my eyes instantly homed in on Gavin fucking King. I'd seen him shirtless before. I was sure that I had, but all previous interactions fled my mind as he walked toward our cabana in nothing but pink trunks that showed off his muscular thighs and revealed every toned inch of abdomen. My mouth went dry.

"Or are you?" English muttered under her breath.

And I had no answer to that.

4

WHITLEY

We spent the rest of the week by the pool, enjoying our time together as we waited for Katherine and Camden to get into town. After a few days, I'd completely lost my melancholic mood. I felt more and more that what I'd done was the absolute right decision. I hadn't realized that my wings had been clipped until now.

Now, I was utterly and entirely myself again.

While we'd congregated in each other's rooms and gone on a few trips into Old San Juan, it was finally the weekend, which meant clubbing. This felt like my best opportunity to meet someone. The resort wouldn't open to the public until after New Year's. So far, it was only available for the uber rich who could afford the exclusivity of the prerelease accommodations. Which was, thus far, limiting my holiday-fling objective.

Tonight, it was back on.

As long as I wasn't too drunk.

Which was going to be a problem.

I showered and diffused my beachy waves, and then I changed into a crop top and miniskirt. I was considering downing an entire bottle of water because, holy shit, I was a little tipsier than I'd thought I'd be, but I also didn't want to have to pee all night either. Oh, the dilemma.

I drank half of it and then took it with me as I headed back out onto the stone path. I was still a few minutes early before we were all meeting. I glanced over at the villa next door. Gavin was getting ready inside. Well, knowing him, he'd already be ready and drinking.

I chewed on my lip and then traipsed down the stone walk. The door was wide open when I walked up to the villa.

"Gavin?" I called. He wasn't anywhere visible as I stepped tentatively across the threshold. "You in here?"

My feet stilled as I moved deeper into the bedroom. The outdoor shower was on. I hadn't been able to hear that from the front door. And now, I was in a perfect position to look out the bedroom window and to the outdoor area, which consisted of a personal pool with lounge chairs and the aforementioned outdoor shower.

Which was on.

And Gavin was in it.

Naked.

I gaped at the sight before me. Water ran down his glorious body from head to toe. My eyes lingered on the hard contours of his back, over his narrow hips, and to his perfect ass. My body heated at his nakedness. That should have been enough to heat me up all on its own. But it was what he was *doing* in the shower, outside, all alone that made me freeze entirely.

He had his dick in his hand, and he was pumping it furiously. His other hand was braced against the wooden enclosure, as if he were a fighter, beat down and debating on going back in the ring. Only he was fighting with himself ... with his cock as he jerked off.

A flush rushed through my body. Holy fuck. He was ... huge. I mean, well, I'd seen a good amount of dick in my days, and Gavin was the biggest I'd seen. Like ... okay, whoa. I needed to stop that train of thought.

My mouth went dry as he sped up. His hand moving with renewed vigor. His stance spread, and his body shook with the exertion. Water ran down his back, darkening his brown-red hair and plastering it forward over his brow, which was furrowed in concentration. Or perhaps ... more. His eyes were closed, and his mouth was open just enough to form a word. Though I couldn't make out what prayer he was saying.

But to my trained eye, he looked close to finishing. Close to unleashing. And already, I had seen too much. My panties were now wet with desire as I watched him pleasure himself. My heart raced in my chest.

I wanted Gavin King. I wanted him precisely as he was now.

Unabashedly sexy and this close to orgasm.

I nearly tripped on my own feet as I retreated backward. I caught myself on his desk and then darted back outside. I shouldn't have watched that. I shouldn't have seen as much as I had. But it was difficult to keep my feet rooted, knowing he was coming in that shower.

My breathing was ragged as I hung on the front door, and I put a hand to my chest to feel my runaway heartbeat. All I could concentrate on was the pulse of my core. I could have made *myself* come in a matter of seconds. I wasn't sure that I would be able to get off later without thinking about what I'd just seen.

The image of Gavin King jacking off in the shower would forever be seared on my brain.

When my body finally settled down and I heard the unmistakable sound of the shower shutting off, I rapped loudly on the front door. "Gavin?"

"Whit?"

"Hey, yeah, it's me."

There was a pause, and then he came out of the bathroom in nothing but a towel. He towel-dried his hair, so it stuck up in all the right places. Then, when he finished, he smirked at me. I admitted that he was really fucking gorgeous. And a few minutes ago, seeing him walk out like this might have made me weak in the knees, but considering what I'd accidentally walked in on ...

"You ready to go?" he asked.

"Uh, yep ... yeah, just came to get you."

"Well, you've got me."

My eyes lowered to his dick, which was covered by the scrap of towel. I jerked my eyes back up. "Thought you'd be ready to go."

"I just have to throw some clothes on. Are you here to watch?"

"Uh ..." My eyes widened. Welp, I had just gotten a show. "Nope. Just here for ..."

Gavin arched an eyebrow. "You seem jumpy."

I swallowed, and my eyes veered lower and lower to that towel again. Fuck. I looked up into his eyes. "I'll just, uh, let you get dressed."

He laughed. "It's just a towel, Whit."

Fuck, I couldn't keep this up. And anyway, he deserved to know that I'd seen him. I didn't want secrets between us. I released a breath. "Well, I ... might have walked inside, thinking you were already ready."

Gavin tilted his head. "Yeah?"

"Uh-huh. You were not finished yet."

"And what exactly did you see?"

I bit my lip. "You know what I saw."

"Never knew you to be shy," he teased.

And I never had been. If he wasn't taking it seriously, then I didn't have to either. So, I sauntered right up to Mr. Tall, Dark, and Shirtless, ran a finger down his still-bare, wet chest, and fluttered my eyelashes. "Do you want me to tell you I saw you jacking off?"

His breath hitched. He'd forgotten for a moment who he was talking to. I *never* backed down from a challenge.

"And did you stay and watch?" he teased right back.

I leaned into the suggestion, my hand still on his chest. "What if I did? Who exactly were you thinking about in there, King?"

His hand wrapped around my wrist. "What if I said you?"

He was joking. *Of course* he was joking. Just playing into this silly, flirtatious game.

"I'd call you a liar, but nice try at your attempt to one-up me."

A muscle feathered in his jaw, but otherwise, he said nothing. I broke from his touch, flipped my hair over my shoulder, and sauntered to the door.

"Get dressed, Gavin. We're going hunting tonight."

5

GAVIN

Watching Whitley strut out of my bedroom after admitting to watching me jack off made me consider going back out to that outdoor shower to pound out another one. Or maybe throwing her over my shoulder to get this out of my goddamn system.

Because *fuck. me.*

I *had* been thinking about her.

I certainly hadn't been lying about a damn thing. All week, she'd been in the skimpiest bikinis imaginable. I'd watched with hungry eyes as she simpered and flirted and played coy. As she talked about this vacation fling that she wanted. And I wasn't about to deny that I would be perfectly happy to fill that position if she was taking requests. If I thought she was actually interested and wouldn't just laugh at me, maybe I'd even offer.

But even now, she'd laughed when I suggested I was thinking about her. That I'd acted like we were just trying to one-up each other rather than telling her the truth. I wanted her. And it was getting harder by the day to deny it.

"You coming?" Whit called from the pathway.

I growled under my breath and threw on a pair of slacks and a button-up. I slicked some gel into my hair and then rolled up the sleeves as I exited the villa. "Ready."

"You men. So quick," she said. But she caught sight of me, and her eyes drifted lower. Maybe she wasn't completely unaffected by seeing me in that shower.

I winked at her. "I'm not always quick. Sometimes, I like to take my time."

She laughed, but it was throaty, and her eyes darted away. "I bet."

"Shall we?"

"We shall."

We walked across the stone pathway and through the flame-lit pool space. Everything flickered and glowed as the sun sank below the horizon. Our friends waited for us on the terrace. I couldn't deny that the six of us looked like a set. Except that Whitley and I were single and not a set at all.

English pulled Whit into a hug. "You look gorgeous."

"Thanks. You too. I am ready to finally get in there!"

Lark laughed. "You're such a heartbreaker."

"Not if I can help it," she said.

"Let's take a picture to taunt Katherine," English said.

"She already hates us for being here without her. Why not?" Lark agreed.

English pulled her phone out and took a selfie with us. She jotted out a text as we all headed inside the nightclub. Music pounded relentlessly as we were escorted to a VIP booth at the back of the club. The nightclub was open to anyone who ventured out to the island. So, Saturday night, it was *packed*. I was glad for the distraction from Whitley swishing her ass back and forth in front of me.

"I would have thought you'd make your move already, Gavin," Court said with a nudge as we followed the girls.

"What move?"

Sam just glanced at me. "We're not stupid."

"I beg to differ."

Court laughed. "Is it going to be tonight then? You're eye-fucking her ass right now."

I jerked my head upward. "I wouldn't do that to Robert."

"To Robert? She's so over him."

"He's not over her."

Sam shrugged. "Since when are you a gentleman?"

Excellent question. The answer was, never. I'd

never been a gentleman. It was why Court, Camden, and I had gotten along in college. Between the three of us, we could get any girl in Cambridge. Now, Camden was married, and I'd bet Court was well on his way. I was the only one left who was a rake through and through. I always took what I wanted when I wanted and fuck the consequences. Why was this different?

Whitley was over Robert. That was more than clear. She'd been flirting with me relentlessly since we'd gotten here, like she had before she started dating him. Was this my cue to go for it?

I sank into a seat, and our bartender scurried up to my side. She was nearly as short as Whitley with flaming-red hair to her cinched-in waist. She wore tight white shorts and a crop that accented her brown skin.

She leaned in. "*Ay, papi*. What can I get you?"

"Shots," Whitley said, dropping down on the other side of the bartender. The bartender swiveled to face her, and Whit gave her best come-hither look. "For both of us."

"Anything in particular?"

Whit met my eye and arched an eyebrow.

"Your call," I told her.

"Tequila," she told the woman. "And what's your name?"

"Patricia." She tucked a lock of hair behind her ear and giggled at Whitley's attention.

"Get one for yourself too, Patricia."

She laughed. "You got it."

When she stepped back to make our drinks, I drew closer to Whit. "What do you think you're doing?"

She put her hand under her chin. The mask of innocence. "Me?"

"Yes, you."

"Well, the bartender is hot. And don't I deserve someone hot, King?"

Yes. Yes, she did.

"Can we share?" I teased.

She looked up, as if she was considering it. I'd heard enough of her wild stories to know that it wouldn't be her first time in a threesome. Certainly wouldn't be mine.

"Do you think you're that lucky?"

I grinned. "Definitely."

Patricia returned in that moment, dropping our shots on the table. "Cheers."

We all three downed our shots as one. Patricia winked at Whit and then headed over to get more drinks for the rest of the booth.

"I won that round," Whit said. She leaned back, as if satisfied from one wink.

"Ha!" I said dramatically. "We have a long way to go before we decide that. I can definitely still land her."

"Oh yeah?" she asked, her caramel hair falling forward like a curtain. "Want to bet on that?"

When the person I wanted was right in front of me,

betting I could get other people was pure stupidity. But I saw the challenge in Whitley's eyes. She liked the idea of us fighting over people. I had a feeling that she liked the push and pull I gave her as much as the teasing and joking.

"I don't think you could keep up," I said, purposely provoking her.

She laughed. "Oh, I bet I can get way more action than you."

"Phone numbers," I suggested. "Whoever has more by the end of the night wins."

She laughed. "Old school."

"It'll even the odds. I bet you can get a dozen guys to Snap you."

"As if I'm only going after guys."

"That does put you at an advantage. I'm straight."

She rolled her eyes and patted my cheek once. "Sure you are."

"You think everyone is a little bit gay."

"Aren't they? How could other girls not look at this and think, *Damn*?" she said, standing and gesturing to herself. Then, she tugged me to my feet. "And guys not look at you and go, *Yeah, I'd jack him off in the shower*?"

I nearly choked on her words. "Is that what *you* thought?"

Her eyebrows shot up, and her mouth fell open slightly, as if she'd been caught red-handed. Then, she winked at me. "Who wouldn't?"

I grinned devilishly because she'd admitted it. Fuck, this was going to be a mistake. But oh well. I was too far in already.

So, I did a stupid thing.

I held my hand out and said, "All right. You're on."

6

WHITLEY

"Thanks, sugar," I said, pressing a pink kiss to the napkin the girl had just given me. "I'll call you."

She giggled and glanced behind her. I'd lost her name in the haze of alcohol. She was one of those who was here with her girlfriends. They were all scouting for hot, available men. This one hadn't admitted her attraction to other girls and kept making sure they hadn't noticed. I was certain she had a crush on the blonde behind her, and, damn, did I hope that she got enough courage after this to ask her out.

I held up the napkin at her as I stepped away. I stuffed it into the small clutch I'd brought with me and sauntered back toward the booth. It was nearly bar close. Our friends had ditched twenty minutes ago to finish their own fun evening. It was just me and Gavin and Patricia at this point.

He was still talking her up when I walked up with my last number of the evening. A pang of something like jealousy flared through me at the way he spoke to Patricia. Was I jealous that Patricia was talking to him or that he was talking to Patricia? It was absurd either way. I was not the jealous type. I was the *sharing is caring* type.

"That's lucky number thirteen," I said as I dropped into Gavin's lap and waved the napkin in his face.

His hands came to my hips as he drew me in closer. "Damn, that's impressive."

"You'd be nothing without me, King," I informed him. "There's a reason I'm your best wingman."

Patricia pushed another round of tequila shots toward us. "So, do you two do this often?"

I reached for my drink. "Do what?"

"Play games in your relationship."

I gaped for a second, glad I hadn't taken the shot while she answered. "Oh, we're not together."

Patricia glanced at Gavin and then back to me. "You're joking."

Gavin shook his head. "Nope. Just friends."

"Sorry. I thought you were in an open relationship. My friend and her boyfriend do this sort of thing to find someone to bring into the relationship sometimes."

I laughed and replayed the night from her perspective. I'd always come back to wave napkins in his face. To show off the new number added to my phone. We'd been teasing each other all night. I was currently lounging in his lap like I belonged there. And, yeah, I was pretty drunk, but this was just who Gavin and I were. We'd always been like this. But apparently, even from a stranger, it looked like more.

"No need to apologize," Gavin said. "Easy mistake."

"We certainly don't look like normal friends," I said. I ran my hand up through his hair and jerked on it lightly to make him look at me. He was drunk, too, but with that one motion, I could feel ... well, fuck, I could feel him stiffen under me. "Do we, baby?"

"I suppose we do not," he allowed.

"Well, if you're looking for a third," Patricia said, suddenly shy, "count me in."

Then, she headed back to the bar to clean up her space. As if to give *us* space to figure out what we wanted.

"There you go," I said playfully. "We have a third. Which I think gives me fourteen and you?"

"I lost count," he said with a shrug. "You win."

"Of course I do."

He hadn't moved away. In fact, his grip on me only tightened. He was hard under my ass. I could shift just a little to feel the entire length of him pressed against me. I heated up at the thought. I could handle my liquor, so even after this much alcohol, I was still cognizant enough to know that this might change everything. That it might even be a bad idea.

I had thirteen phone numbers. Fourteen offers. And somehow, the one I wanted was right in front of my face.

"And what do I win?" I asked, the words coming out breathier than I'd intended.

His eyes dipped to my lips and back up. "What do you want?"

That was as much of an invitation as I'd ever heard.

Our eyes were locked. Emerald green on my hazel. Something passed between us. This was our line. We could cross it with so little effort. All I had to do was shift on his cock. To run my hand through his hair. To claim his soft, pouty lips. He didn't even need to run a hand under my skirt to discover my arousal. I was sure he could sense it as I held perfectly still and lingered on the outline of his lips. On the cusp of the opportunity that presented itself.

He didn't say anything as the choice lay at my feet. Just watched and waited.

I'd taken Gavin's behavior at face value. He was flirtatious. Obviously, he found me attractive, but he'd never made it seem like he was interested in me. Our personalities were too similar. Too friendly and joking and over the top. He took what he wanted from models and celebrities and socialites on the scene back home.

He'd never acted like he was going to take anything from me.

Now, I looked at the past year from that outside perspective Patricia had given me. I hadn't wanted to screw up what was here. Maybe Gavin hadn't either.

And the question was, if I said yes, would it fuck everything up?

I was the queen of compartmentalizing my life. Sex was sex was sex. It didn't have to mean anything. It certainly didn't have to include feelings.

But it was complicated with friends. And friends with benefits *never* worked. No matter how anyone else said it would be fine, someone always caught feels, and someone always got hurt.

"Is this going to ruin everything?" I asked, putting the truth out in front of us.

His hand slipped through my light-brown hair, brushing a strand of it behind my ear. I shivered at the touch. "No."

"How can you know?"

He cupped the back of my neck. Then, he pulled me forward until our lips nearly touched. I shivered all over.

"Whitley, what do you *want*?"

"This," I gasped.

Because when he commanded it out of me, I could deny him nothing.

And in that moment, he knew. Just as I knew. I wanted this to happen. This *was* happening.

His lips crushed to mine, and the entire nightclub disappeared in a haze. He tasted like a mix of tequila and lime. Underneath it all was that pure male taste of him. Just Gavin. Our tongues brushed together, a clash, a sigh, a reprieve. As if every second before this had been the buildup to this collision.

In that moment, I was lost.

One cruel kiss had sundered me.

7

WHITLEY

We crashed into Gavin's villa like a tornado. Hands grasping, lips crushed together, bodies hot and needy.

Gavin kicked the door closed behind him. It made a reverberating noise from the violent shove he'd given it. He reached for me. All five feet of me as he bent forward to get to my lips again.

"Fuck, you're so tiny," he ground out.

"You're not," I teased. My hands skimmed down the front of his shirt to the waist of his pants.

"Yeah?" He smirked. "That what you actually saw in the shower that got you all flustered?"

"I wasn't flustered." I snapped the button on his pants.

"You could barely form coherent sentences."

"You were stroking your cock. What the fuck did you expect me to do?"

"Join me," he growled.

My knees nearly buckled at the hot intensity in that statement. My eyes slid to his as I drew the zipper to the base of his pants. "Is that what you wanted?"

He brushed his tongue along my bottom lip before sliding it all the way in my mouth. We tangled, and I held the edge of his pants as if I might topple over.

"Yes."

He pressed another kiss to my lips. A challenge in those bright green eyes. The light caught on the dark ends of his hair, highlighting the red undertones. I loved a challenge. I loved the drunk taste of him. The hot feel of him. And, damn, did I want to prove to him that I could take anything head-on.

I dragged a finger down the front of his pants, where his cock was currently stretching the material. He pushed forward into my hand, and I palmed him through his pants. Now that I had a hand on him, I could really gather just how huge he was. Small hands hadn't mattered in medical school. It didn't matter when I was performing surgery. It certainly wouldn't matter here. Except ... maybe I wouldn't be able to wrap my hand all the way around him.

"Fuck, Whit." His hands tightened in my hair, and he dragged my lips back to his. "These fucking lips. Dick-sucking lips."

I choked out a laugh at the words that had been uttered in my presence so often in my life. My clients frequently said they wanted lips like mine and asked how many syringes I used to achieve that result. But these were all natural.

"Sounds like you've been thinking about that one," I teased.

"I've wondered what your lips would feel like around my cock since the day I met you."

My eyes flared wide. "Really?"

He nipped at my enlarged lower lip. "Show me."

I smirked defiantly. Then, I slid my hands under the waist of his boxers and slipped them down his thighs. His cock jutted forward, long and hard between us. He was so much taller than me that it came to my fucking stomach. There was no way I was going to be able to get on my knees here.

I pushed him backward and kicked the chair out. He sank into it, tugging his pants the rest of the way off. I wrapped my hand around him and pumped up and down, the way I'd seen him do in the shower.

His head fell backward, and a breath of air escaped him. "Fuck."

"Were you really thinking about me in the shower?"

My lips came to the head of his cock. I stared down at it for a second, fortifying myself for what was to come. Then, my lips spread around the head of him, and I brought him into my mouth.

He groaned, deep and throaty, as he said, "Yes."

"Doing this?"

"Sinking into your cunt."

My body hummed at the filthy words. They should have turned me off, but on my knees before Gavin King, I couldn't feel any shame. I was worshipping a King after all.

I bobbed up and down on his cock as I used my hand to reach the base. There was no way that I was going to get him all the way in my mouth. Not tonight at least. Not without some work. Not that he seemed to give a fuck. If anything, it seemed he was struggling to keep from jerking up into me.

I felt ... powerful.

Blow jobs, when done correctly, were the most powerful act on the planet. It was all about conquering men who thought they were in control. But Gavin succumbed to me. My DSLs being put to good work.

"Fuck, fuck, fuck," he said as he thrust upward.

I choked a little on the length of him and pulled back. His eyes were wanton as they latched back on mine. Then, whatever control he had yielded snapped back to him. He righted himself, lifting me effortlessly over his shoulder like a barbarian.

I gasped as he carried me the rest of the way across

the villa. My ass was entirely on display as his arm was strapped across my legs.

"Gavin!" I cried out before he unceremoniously dumped me onto the king-size bed.

He grinned that wicked smile. "I was right, you know?"

I slid back on the bed, stretching sexily. "About what?"

"Your lips were perfection."

I colored at the compliment. I knew I gave good head. I'd heard that before, but hearing it from Gavin, as his eyes stripped me bare, was a whole new experience. Gavin, who saw me for exactly who I was and liked every bit of it. Gavin, who never made fun of my antics. Gavin, who always endeavored to make them more dramatic. He didn't have to try to make me feel easy about being around him. We just fit.

I'd assumed it was always going to be as friends. But here, now, as he towered over me, I wondered if this had been inevitable. If I'd always been waiting for us to get to this moment.

I'd wanted a vacation fling. Gavin was ... so much more than that.

He grabbed a condom from his bag and slid it on the length of him. He tossed the wrapper and crawled onto the bed after me.

"Fuck, I want you."

"How do you want me?" I teased.

He arched an eyebrow. "What's your favorite position?"

"What's yours?"

At the same time, we said, "Doggy."

He grabbed my hips in his hands and flipped me over. I squeaked at the sudden movement before pushing my ass backward toward him. To my surprise, he didn't thrust right inside and take what I was offering.

He bent down and pressed a kiss to one side of my ass and then one on the other. He spread my cheeks wider, revealing my black thong. Two fingers trailed down the center of me—from my asshole down to my awaiting pussy.

"Are you ready for me?"

I groaned as he slid aside the thong and dragged those fingers through the wet center of me. "Oh God."

He pushed inside of me, and I tightened all around him. My eyes closed as he took his time, exploring my pussy.

"So wet, Whit."

"Please," I gasped.

Normally, I liked a good long foreplay. Lots of orgasms from being eaten out. But right now, I could practically come just from him touching me. Him manhandling me in ways that hadn't been done to me ... maybe ever. I'd always had such a dominating personality that most people let me take control where I wanted. Gavin was not that person.

Finally, he removed his fingers and slipped my panties over my hips. He lifted my body up, so I was on all fours. "This what you wanted?"

"God, yes," I said.

Then, he slammed inside of me. I rocked forward, nearly losing my balance. He stretched and stretched and stretched me, and, fuck, he wasn't even all the way in. I was so fucking warmed up, yet still, he moved forward.

"Oh my god, Gavin. How fucking big are you?"

He laughed, a confident know-it-all laugh. "Is that a complaint?"

He pushed in further, and I saw stars.

"Definitely no."

"I'd say I'll take it slow," he said as he gripped my hips and pulled me another inch backward onto him, "but I don't think you want me to."

One more inch, and finally—*finally*—he was inside of me. We both moaned at the relief. I was as full as I'd ever been in my life. Stuffed full in the best way possible. My pussy contracted around him, wanting him exactly where he was.

"That's right," he said, tightening his grip on my hips.

Then, he started moving. And true to his word, he was not slow. His rhythm was instantly hot and fast. I held on for dear life as I pushed myself backward into each thrust. Harder with every push. My body could barely contain itself from all the feelings all at once.

Everything else fell away. The entire world narrowed to this one moment. I'd had partners before Gavin, but none could compare to exactly how I was feeling. Everything coalesced into one unforgettable orgasm that rocked through my body, completely unprompted.

I cried out as he continued to drive deep into me. But my tightening triggered his own, and he plunged down one more time before stilling as he emptied himself.

My name was a murmur, a whisper, a prayer on his lips as he came. "Whit, Whit, Whit."

I dropped forward onto my elbows, as my hands could no longer support me. He withdrew, slow and steady, and the rest of my body followed.

I threw my arms wide and stared at him in awe. "What did you do to me?"

He smirked as he discarded the condom. Then, he crawled back onto the bed and pulled my small body into his. "Exactly what you wanted me to."

Then, he kissed my shoulder, and we both promptly fell into a heavy, dreamless sleep.

8

GAVIN

The next morning, I was stolen from a perfect dream.

In the dream, I'd made a bet with a pixie. And when she'd won, she'd stolen my heart for the night.

But when I cracked my eyes open, the pixie slept soundly next to me.

Her caramel hair was a wave around her head. Her plump lips invitingly half-open. Her breasts had been released from her top at some point in the night. We were both naked, and already, my body was responding to her ass pressed hard against me.

It hadn't been a dream at all.

Whitley and I had slept together last night, and here, in the light of day, she was still in my bed.

As much as I wanted to stay in this moment forever, I tugged on a pair of boxers and padded into the bathroom. After relieving myself, I brushed my teeth and then hopped into the shower. We'd passed out, sweaty and exhausted, last night. I had no complaints. None at all. But I was a *shower in the morning* kind of guy, and routine took over.

I considered calling for room service. We could stay in bed all morning and forget about the rest of the world. None of our friends would care if we ditched until lunch, right?

I'd just been contemplating an omelet when I heard the bed creak from the other room. Whitley had her clothes back on and was looking around the room, wide-eyed.

"Morning," I said, leaning against the bathroom door.

Her head whipped to the side, and she relaxed when she saw I was still there. "Hey."

"You want anything for breakfast? I was thinking of ordering in."

"Oh," she said softly. "Um ... actually, I was going to go back to my room."

I saw it then. Fear. She had the look of a trapped bird, trying to escape the coop. I'd never seen Whitley look at me like that before, but I'd certainly seen her look like that when she was interested in someone else.

"You don't have to go."

She tucked a lock of her hair behind her ear, which

was wild from the salty Caribbean air. "Gavin, I ... this ..."

She couldn't seem to string her words together. But I knew what she was going to say. *It shouldn't have happened. It was too soon. This was just a fling, a one-time thing.* It didn't sting any less.

Of course, it was exactly what I should have expected. It was how both Whitley and I always operated. Plus, she had just gotten out of a serious relationship. With one of my best friends.

Fuck, I was an idiot.

"You don't have to explain," I said quickly. The last thing I wanted was for her to be uncomfortable after the incredible night we'd had. "I know that you and Robert just broke up."

Her eyes widened a fraction, and then she nodded. "Robert ... right."

"And you wanted a vacation fling."

"I did." She chewed on her bottom lip. The lips I'd fantasized about and discovered they were way better than even my imagination. "I really didn't mean to put you in this position, Gavin."

"What position?"

She looked down and then away. "You know, Robert's your friend."

"He is, but ..."

"And he doesn't have to know."

I closed my mouth on that. *He doesn't have to know.*

Oh shit, I'd definitely misinterpreted all of this. She wanted it to be a secret. She didn't want anyone to know.

"I don't want to come between friends. Lark told us what happened with Penn and Natalie, and I don't want that for y'all," she said, a hint of her Southern accent peeking out. She always tried so hard to hide her roots. That she'd slipped was admission enough that this had rattled her.

"You won't come between us."

"Good," she said on a breath of relief. "So ... we can stay friends?"

Friends.

It felt like a gut punch. But, fuck, it must be what she wanted. Last night had been incredible. I'd wanted it for a long time. I couldn't actually imagine never having it again. I wasn't going to force the girl to see my side though.

"If that's what you want," I offered.

She nodded and took a step toward the door. "It's probably for the best. Right? We just got carried away last night with the bet and the drinking and dancing."

And *fucking*.

We'd made no promises. We'd never said exactly what this was. We'd just lived in the moment. And I couldn't regret a single thing. Not a single thing. Even if it was the last time it would happen.

"We said it wouldn't ruin everything," she

reminded me. The words she'd uttered last night before the kiss that changed everything.

Maybe that had been a promise.

And I was a fool.

I'd thought she meant that it wouldn't ruin *us*. But she meant Robert. She meant our friendship. I didn't clarify. I didn't even ask her to be more specific. I'd just demanded what she wanted, and when she said me, I'd thrown the whole rulebook out the window.

But I was the player. I could handle this. I'd gotten my shot with her. And now, it was over. At least now, I knew.

"It won't ruin anything."

She nodded. "Good. I just think we should act like nothing has changed."

"Okay." Except that everything had changed.

"I'll just ..." She gestured to the door. "I'll see you later."

"All right."

She was halfway out the door before I followed after her. I leaned against the doorframe and watched her take the stairs.

"Whit," I called.

She turned back around in surprise. "Yeah?"

"I had a good time."

Her eyes crinkled at the corners when she smiled. It was almost a shy thing. Not something I'd ever seen from her before. "Me too."

"It's too bad it can't happen again."

She laughed softly and winked at me. Playful Whitley was back in place. Was it a mask, or was this reality?

"It is."

Then, she strolled back to her villa. I ran a hand back through my hair as she disappeared inside.

Fucking fuck.

What the hell just happened?

9

WHITLEY

What the hell just happened?

I fell face-first on the bed with a frustrated groan. Gavin had been so eager to bring up Robert. I'd seen the fear in his eyes that said he didn't want me to ruin his friendship.

I didn't know what I'd just done. All I could think was *panic*. *Don't be the girl who comes between friends. Don't be the girl who hurts people. Don't show them that you care enough about any of it.*

So, basically, my MO.

If you didn't care about anything, then you couldn't get hurt.

Except that I *had* cared about what happened last night with Gavin. I'd lit up in a way that I didn't remember ever doing before. And it was beyond the rocking orgasm. It was something about being with him.

But that *look*.

Ugh!

And then what was that at the end? When he'd said it was too bad it couldn't happen again. *He* was the one who had made it seem like he didn't want it to happen again. Sure, he'd offered me breakfast or whatever, but that was just Gavin.

He didn't want anyone to know. He didn't want it to get back to Robert. So, I'd followed along.

And as much as I wanted to not care, it hurt.

I needed to get it together. Katherine was coming in today, and we had a girls' trip planned.

I'd told Gavin that we could just be friends. That nothing had to change. Just like what he wanted.

I could do that.

I could play the part.

But I needed a shower first.

By the time I headed down to the pool, I'd missed breakfast. I ordered a carb-heavy snack from the waiter, coupled with my standard piña colada, and collapsed next to Lark and English.

"God, I'm tired. I still feel hungover," I complained.

Lark laughed. "Well, you and Gavin were drinking pretty heavily."

"We were."

"How late did you stay out?" English asked.

"Uh, I don't know. To bar close." I really did not want to talk about Gavin King right now. Last night had made me heat up, and this morning had doused me with ice water. It was enough to make any girl have whiplash. I quickly changed the subject. "So, have you heard from Katherine?"

"She got in a few minutes ago," Lark said. "She texted and said she'd meet us poolside. So, here we wait."

"I wonder how her anniversary went," English said.

"How do you *think* it went? She has an arranged marriage, and they practically hate each other," I said.

Lark shook her head. "No, they don't hate each other. There's something there. I just don't know how she deals with it."

"He's an ass, but he's our ass," English said. "He helped me when I had the issue with the publicity firm."

"Yeah."

"And he got Court out of trouble."

I laughed. "*You* got Court out of trouble."

She waved a drink at me. "It's a theme."

"He also helped get Sam a job," Lark said.

"And crushed that horrid ex of yours," I pointed out.

Lark wrinkled her nose. "How could I forget? But regardless, he pushes all of her buttons."

"That can be fun in bed," I said, waggling my eyebrows.

"It can," Lark agreed. "If Katherine would dare to let him."

English grinned devilishly. "All of us would dare to let him if we weren't currently attached."

Lark snorted. "Not me. I grew up on the Upper East Side. I don't go that crazy anymore."

"Anymore, she says," I said with a laugh.

Lark tossed a throw pillow at me. "Hey!"

We all fell into a fit as my nachos, fries, and drink showed up. I tipped the waiter and dug in. I was nearly done with my hangover cure when Katherine Van Pelt herself appeared in all her glory. If I wasn't already sure I was bi, then Katherine would have confirmed that for me. Because, damn, she could wear a bikini.

English jumped up first and pulled her into a hug. Katherine dumped her stuff on a chair, but to our surprise, Camden didn't immediately disappear. In fact, it was weird enough that they'd shown up to the pool together. They never did things together that weren't specifically planned.

Camden asked her about a drink and then attacked her mouth. My eyes widened in shock. Camden Percy initiating public displays of affection. What in the hell was happening?

It wasn't until he left that she came clean.

"Well, we have a sort of ... truce."

"Truce?" Lark prompted.

"Yeah. We're not going to argue at all while we're here. Going to just ... see how it goes."

Lark saw one of her other friends and pulled Katherine over to say hi. English and I exchanged a glance.

"A truce? With *Camden*?" I asked.

She shrugged. "Seems like a recipe for disaster. But what do I know?"

"Maybe it'll be good for her."

"Maybe."

"And what about you?"

"Me?"

English rolled her eyes. "You were flirting with Gavin all night. Don't act so innocent."

"We weren't flirting. We had a bet."

"Yeah, yeah. A bet. As if that isn't flirting with you two."

"What bet?" Katherine asked when she returned a minute later.

"Oh, you'll love this," Lark said. "It's like our old antics."

"Gavin and I had a bet to see who could get the most phone numbers last night. It wasn't anything."

Katherine arched an eyebrow at Lark. "That is much too nice for our old antics."

"True," Lark said with a devious grin. "Our bets were a lot higher stakes."

"Tell me you won," Katherine said. "If you lose bets, you end up married."

Her eyes trailed after her husband. That was a story I'd love to hear.

"I won," I told her confidently.

"What did you win?" she asked.

"More importantly, who did you go home with?" English asked. She shot me a look that said she had guessed right all along about me and Gavin.

But I'd promised Gavin that I wouldn't say anything. He didn't want this to get back to Robert. So, I couldn't even tell my friends.

"Uh, I didn't," I lied. "I was too drunk."

"All those phone numbers and no action?" Lark said. "Doesn't sound like you."

"Well, we have tonight too. Bet some of those people will be back at the club."

Katherine's eyes narrowed marginally. She had a knack for seeing to the heart of people. As if she could just look straight through you, past all the masks you hid behind, and get to the true center.

"Tonight then," she concluded.

"What's happening tonight?" Court asked.

He picked English up like a rag doll and plopped

her into his lap on her chair. She swatted at him but clearly liked the attention.

"We're going to go dancing," Katherine declared.

"Dancing?" Sam shot Lark a questioning look. "Do I have to dance?"

She patted his cheek. "You can sway back and forth. You'll be fine."

Gavin dropped into a seat next to mine. He had on green shorts, the color of his eyes, and when he slouched backward in the seat, holding his beer in front of him, they rode up high on his thighs. My eyes drifted to the exposed tan skin and the hard muscles. He'd used those to thrust inside of me last night. Those long fingers and wide, callous palms to grasp my hips hard enough that I was lucky I didn't have bruises. And hidden by those green shorts was the huge length of him that had practically knocked me out.

My eyes swept upward. He was looking straight at me. He smirked in the flirtiest, Gavin-iest way ever. It said he knew *exactly* what I'd been looking at and precisely what I'd been thinking. My cheeks heated, and I turned back to my drink.

"What about you, Gav?" Court asked. "I know you'll be on the dance floor."

"Definitely," Gavin said. He held his beer bottle up. "Going to get some ass tonight."

"Oh, Gavin," Katherine said. "So discriminating in your attentions. Anything with two legs will do?"

He met Queen Katherine head-on. "And you, *Ren*? Who do you favor tonight? Both of them are here, are they not?"

She tipped her head at his audacity. It was a long-known fact that she'd been in love with Court's brother, but now, they were both married—not to each other, obviously—and living their own lives. It was ballsy of Gavin to even mention it.

"Careful, King," she said.

Court smacked him, nearly knocking the drink out of his hand. "Don't be an ass."

"He can't help it," English said with an eye roll.

His gaze swept back to me as he shrugged. "What can I say? I'm an ass man."

The rest of the group snorted. Typical Gavin antics.

But I felt like we were in a completely different universe. I'd said that I'd be his friend. That no one had to know what had happened. But when he looked at me like that, I was sure everyone could tell exactly what we'd done last night.

I got to my feet, flushed and horny, and headed to the bar for another drink. Gavin followed in my wake. He put in for another beer and leaned against the bar.

"You shouldn't antagonize Katherine," I told him.

He laughed. "She likes when people stand up to her. Why do you think she likes you?" His eyes were on my lips again when I turned to face him. "You seem flustered, Whit."

I swallowed and stepped back. "Me?" I asked, reaching for my bravado again. I grabbed my piña colada and took a good long drink. "Please. What do I have to be flustered about?"

He watched my DSLs suck on that straw with intense interest. "Oh, I can think of a few things."

Just friends. We were just friends.

I said it over and over again as I laughed off his comment and headed back to my friends. Holy fuck. How was I going to survive the rest of the week?

10

GAVIN

When I showed up at the club later that night, the girls were already in attendance. English and Lark were drinking in the booth from the night before. They perked up when they saw their boyfriends enter.

No Katherine or Whitley in sight.

"Where's the rest of your quartet?"

English gave me a knowing look. Had Whit told her? She pointed to the dance floor. I found Katherine immediately. She was being twirled around in some kind of salsa like a professional by a local. But Whitley was harder to find, in that she was in a press of bodies at the heart of the dance floor.

Her hair was down. A shimmery dress barely hit mid-thigh. Her body moved effortlessly to the tempo of the Latin music through the speakers. Some guy had his hands on her while a girl pressed her back to Whitley's chest.

A flare of hot desire shot through me. I wanted to storm over there and steal her away. My hand clenched into a fist. But she didn't want anyone to find out about us, and she'd said we were just friends. Of course she could dance with anyone at the club. Anyone at all.

I hadn't expected this flash of jealousy, but I didn't like to see her out there. I didn't like it at all.

"Drink?" Court asked.

"Sure. Whatever you're having."

I wasn't going to go over there. I might have been flirty this afternoon at the pool. I mean, she'd said that was what she wanted, but I didn't have to make it easy for her, did I? Would dancing push it too far?

Court handed me a rum and Coke. It was a local blend and fucking delicious. I'd had it last night too.

"When is Camden showing?"

Court nearly choked on his drink as he pointed out on the dance floor. "Guess he showed up already."

Camden was staring at Katherine with barely contained control. He was a master of control. So, seeing just a flicker of anything like emotion from him was satisfying. Katherine stilled on the dance floor, and her partner offered her hand to Camden. Yeah, anyone could feel that gaze on them.

Camden tugged her to him with all the dominance he possessed. Katherine, the ice princess herself, actually started to *toy* with him. Lord help her. She tilted her head to the side, and my eyes widened when, a minute later, they just fucking disappeared.

"Did that just happen?" I asked.

"He's got game."

"That is some truce."

Court shrugged. "One of them is going to blow it soon. You can't contain that much roiling anger."

I couldn't argue with him there.

"Dance with me," English said, holding her hand out to Court.

He shot me a look. "I've been summoned."

Lark and Sam followed them out onto the dance floor.

There were a dozen beautiful women that I could dance with. Any one of them would probably be happy to go home with me tonight. I could forget Whitley the old-fashioned way.

And yet ...

My eyes flickered back to where she now danced exclusively with the woman. Whoever the guy was had disappeared. That didn't give me any comfort though. I was just as jealous of the beautiful woman in her arms as the guy. She favored them equally.

"Fuck it," I growled.

We were friends. We'd danced hundreds of times together before we fucked. What was different about tonight?

I downed the rest of my drink and then strode out onto the dance floor. Whitley's arms were high above her head now. She swayed to the music as the woman in front of her bent forward at the waist.

She jumped at the first touch as I circled her wrists and then dragged my hands down her forearms, over her biceps, and to her shoulders. Her eyes flicked backward in surprise. She looked half-ready to tell whoever it was to disappear.

Then, she saw it was me. "Gavin?"

I brushed my lips against the shell of her ear. "Keep dancing."

She opened her mouth as if to argue and then snapped it closed. My hands continued their descent over her waist and to her hips. I kept her hips moving in the tempo she'd been going at the second before I interrupted.

"I don't know if this is a good idea," she said, barely audible over the music.

I jerked her hips backward, harder against me. I was so much taller than her. Even tonight, with four-inch platforms on, she just came up to my shoulder. But that hadn't been a hindrance last night, and it didn't have to be right now.

"We're just dancing," I told her.

She huffed, giving me a disbelieving look.

"We've danced together a hundred times." I spun

her around, drawing her into my arms and stealing her from the woman. "Is this different?"

Her licked a track across her bottom lip. "Just dancing, huh?"

"What else would it be?"

"Oh, I can think of a few things," she shot my words back at me.

I gave her a devilish grin. "Now, whose mind is in the gutter?"

She pulled back, as if she were going to retreat entirely, but I laughed. I put as much flirty teasing tone into it. I didn't want to chase her away, but I wanted this dance. I could tell *she* wanted this dance. She might have said we were just friends, but friends didn't push you down in a chair to suck you off. They didn't fuck. They certainly didn't fall asleep naked in each other's arms.

She didn't want Robert to know. And, fuck, I didn't want him to be upset by this either, but I wasn't ready to walk away.

I grasped her arms and slung them around my neck. It was just like last night. When she'd forced herself backward on my cock as I pushed into her. Every single beat hit at a perfect pace.

"Just a dance?" she asked when that song finished and the next one started. She didn't pull away again though.

"Just a dance."

She nodded and rested her head against my chest. The pixie fit in my arms as if she had been made to be there.

I wanted more, but I wasn't going to force her to give me more than she was ready for. Maybe once we were back from this vacation, we could figure it out.

It didn't have to be today.

I just didn't want it to be never.

11

WHITLEY

A week passed in a flurry of flirty looks. I'd bailed early that night at the club, and we hadn't gone back. But trying to act normal around Gavin was harder than I'd thought it would be.

It was officially New Year's Eve and Katherine's birthday *and* our last night of vacation. I didn't want to stress over any of it. I was determined to just have as much fun as possible. Tomorrow, we'd be back in the city. Reality would return. But tonight, I was free.

I traipsed down the walkway and onto the beach with English at my side. The guys trailed behind us. Lark had planned a special beach party for Katherine. English and I had come down earlier to make sure everything was to Katherine's impossibly high standards. But seeing it now, as the sun set on the water, I was impressed.

"Wow," I whispered.

"Pretty great, right?" English asked.

I nodded. It really was. We'd managed to create a beachside pillow fort with dozens of plush blankets laid out, topped with a veritable mountain of pillows. The beach was already the place to be for the resort's inaugural New Year's Eve event. Bodies moved in time to music a DJ was blasting. A beach volleyball game had started up while there was still light. Luckily, our group had our own bartender.

"This is amazing," Sam said. "Lark had her work cut out for her."

"Hey, we helped!" English argued.

"You did great, babe," Court said, squeezing her ass.

She rolled her eyes at him, and we all settled down in the mass of pillows.

Katherine had a themed black, gold, and silver event. I was in a slinky silver wrap dress, which actually made sitting kind of difficult. English had chosen a black romper that showed off miles of long, tan legs. Arguably, a better choice for a beach party. Lark's red hair would be highlighted in her gold number.

And then Katherine appeared with Lark in tow, and of course—*of course*—she'd broken her own rules. She was in a bright red dress. It was gorgeous on her and made her stand out, which was likely the point.

We were only missing Camden. Surely, he wouldn't skip his own wife's birthday.

"Happy birthday!" we all cheered as she joined the group.

"Thank you. This is perfect. Almost as good as if I'd done it myself."

Lark laughed at her. "You perfectionist."

"Control freak," English added.

"But you're *our* perfectionist control freak," I said with a smile.

Katherine arched an eyebrow at all of us and took an offered drink. "That sounds accurate."

"All right. Enough chitchatting. Let's dance!" I downed my drink and pointed straight at Gavin.

We were the only ones not coupled up. I didn't plan to sit around all night. This was nothing out of the ordinary. I could lie to myself just fine.

Gavin arched his eyebrows and gestured to himself. "Me?"

"Yeah, you," I said with a grin. "Come dance with me."

He laughed, but I saw a glint of something else in his eyes. Desire. I shivered at that look.

He stepped across the blankets. "All right, bossy."

I looked right back at him, defiance in my expression. "Bossy girls are just leaders who didn't stay down when boys told them to be quiet."

He smirked then, roguish and handsome in the firelight. "By all means, lead then."

I winked at my friends and then dragged him into the crowd. Probably, this was stupid. But, god, I wanted to have fun. Gavin was fun. It didn't have to mean anything ... right?

"What's this, Whit?" he asked as I pushed into the throng.

"This is dancing. You're good at it."

"So are you."

"Exactly. Let's just have fun, Gavin," I begged of him. "I feel like since we slept together, things have been so ... tense. I am not a tense person. I can't live in a world of angst." He chuckled at my words. "I'm serious. I want to spend the night with my friends and dance the night away. Can we do that?"

"We can do that," he confirmed as his hands came to my hips.

We got lost in the music. It was exhilarating to be just a number in the crowd. And then all of our friends were there with us. A pop song came on, and all of us sang at the top of our lungs. Katherine made a joke about how good my singing voice was. I'd always been self-conscious of my voice. Not that I was bad. I was good. Really good. But my parents hated the talent for no particular reason. They wanted a smart daughter, not one chasing after a musical dream that had such a small chance of success. I'd hidden it for so long that I didn't know how to find my voice. Even though I was always the life of the party.

I avoided Katherine's questioning look by grabbing Gavin's shirt in both hands and dragging him against me.

"What was that about?" he asked, his lips tauntingly close.

"Nothing."

"You have a great voice."

I shrugged. "So does everyone."

He laughed. "No, they don't. You should sing more."

"Nah. It's just for fun."

"And what are we doing tonight?" he teased.

I opened and closed my mouth. Well, wasn't he sneaky? Yes, tonight, we were just having fun.

So, I sang to him. Just him. Not loud enough for anyone else to hear like before. His eyes lit up as I serenaded him through the next couple songs. A slow song came on, and I crooned the seductive tones.

"Jesus Christ, that's sexy," he breathed into my ear.

"The dancing or the lyrics?"

"You."

I shivered all over at that word. I'd never used my voice to seduce anyone. Not like this. And I felt sexy, just hearing him praise me. Like my voice wasn't just my secret, but now, it was *our* secret. Another secret. I liked this one just as much.

"Come on. There's cake," Lark called, gesturing for us to head back to our blankets.

Gavin grabbed my hand with his and threaded us through the crowd. I flopped down at the edge of the group with Gavin taking the seat next to me. We weren't quite touching, but we weren't exactly subtle either.

The cake was a three-tiered beauty that ombréd from blood red to pink with a tiara candle at the top. It was a confectionary masterpiece. Katherine took up position before it. Camden was at her side. I'd missed when he showed, but the smile painted on Katherine's mouth said that she was pleased by the appearance. Good for them. I hoped we were all wrong and this truce was exactly what they needed.

We sang "Happy Birthday," and as the song ended, I called out, "Make a wish!"

Gavin nudged me, and I laughed, mouthing *What?* as I leaned into him.

He wrapped a seemingly casual arm around my waist. As Katherine made her wish and blew out the candle, all I could think about was that arm. How easily it had slipped into place. How right I felt, lying against him.

"Want to go back and dance?" he asked.

I glanced back at him. Our lips were lined up, so I barely had to breathe to reach them. I swallowed hard and tried to remind myself this was just fun. No angst. No drama. Just fun.

"Sure."

He grinned. His eyes slipped down to my lips and then back up. It was a fraction of a second, but it was clear we were both thinking the same thing.

"Coming?" Lark asked.

I jerked away from Gavin as if we'd been caught kissing. Lark gave me a knowing look and offered me a hand. I took it to get up out of the sand.

"You two looked comfy," she said with a smile.

"He is comfy," I said with a laugh. "Everyone needs a big, strong man to lie on like a pillow."

Lark laughed. "If you say so."

Gavin followed behind us, and we fell into the crowd again. It was nearly midnight. A countdown blasted the last two minutes as we danced crazily to the music. Gavin tugged me against him as we hit the final minute.

"What's your resolution?" he asked me.

"I don't believe in them."

"No?"

"Do the best you can all year long. That's all that matters."

"Did you do the best you could this year? In this last minute?"

I bit my lip. "I think so."

"Well, I can think of one more thing I'd like to do."

He tilted my chin up until I looked deep into his green eyes as the final ten seconds were cheered behind us.

"What's that?" I breathed.

"Three, two, one! Happy New Year!" everyone shouted all around us.

"This."

Then, Gavin's lips touched mine, heralding in the new year.

12

GAVIN

Whitley's body went rigid and her lips immobile. For a split second, I feared that she'd pull away. We'd agreed after all that we wouldn't keep doing this.

But then she went pliant. A shudder of relief filtered through me as she pressed her body against mine, wrapped her arms around my neck, and sealed our lips together. I groaned deep in the back of my throat and lifted her effortlessly out of the sand. She grinned against my lips, but I kept kissing her, tasting the fruity drink on her tongue and the week of want that hung heavy between us.

I finally set her back down on her feet. She swayed slightly, as if I'd made her legs wobbly from one kiss.

"I thought we were just having fun," she teased.

I pressed another kiss to her pretty pink lips. "This is fun."

"You're a scoundrel. I thought you didn't want Robert to know."

"*You* didn't want Robert to know."

"No, but *you* said that."

I shook my head. "No, you just got out of a relationship. I didn't want you to be uncomfortable, knowing Robert and I are friends."

"Will you still be friends if he finds out?"

I had no answer to that. "You and I don't have to do this if that's what *you* want. But not out of an obligation to someone else."

In response, she stood on her tiptoes and brought my lips back down to hers. I kissed her long and hard, careless of who else saw. No one had to know. Everyone could know. Whatever she wanted. As long as I got her one more night. I couldn't survive not getting another taste of her.

"Let's get out of here."

I reached for her hand, and as she had all night, she let me guide her out of the mass of people. Our friends would wonder where we'd gone off to, but I hoped they were enjoying themselves enough right now not to think too much on it. We still had a lot of unanswered questions about what was happening. But they could wait for another day.

We threaded our fingers together as we ducked

away from the New Year's Eve party. Last time we'd done this, we had been in too much of a hurry. We'd decided on a drunk whim to give in to temptation. Now, our arms swung in an easy rhythm, hands locked between us as we walked on the cobbled path that led to our villas.

Silence lingered, but it was far from uncomfortable. It felt almost natural. Even though neither of us was particularly the quiet type. Whitley was as fun and boisterous and outspoken as they came, and I always had a careful quip for the situation. But here, there was no posturing.

It was nice for a change.

"Your place or mine?"

She tilted her head to the side and then said, "Yours."

"Mine it is."

We headed up the short set of stairs and then inside. She lingered on the threshold for a second, as if she couldn't believe she was doing this.

"Whit?"

Her eyes jumped to mine. "Just didn't think I'd be here again."

"If you're uncertain ..."

"No," she said automatically. "It's strange actually. I have no uncertainty."

"Why is that strange? You're always overly confident."

She walked over the entranceway and closed the door behind her. "I might appear that way, but I'm not. I don't think anyone is as confident as they portray."

"Maybe."

"I just ... I'm not good at this. At the second night. The second date. Any kind of real relationship. I'm the bad girlfriend that parents warn you about."

I smirked. "I'm pretty sure I was not warned off anyone like you."

Her eyes crinkled at the edges. "You'd be surprised."

"You haven't met my family."

The Kings were ... notorious. Old Texas oil money sure had a reputation. That was all I was saying.

"I don't feel uncertainty toward you, King," she said, running her hands up the front of my linen shirt. She gripped the open collar, as she'd done in the sand, and drew me closer to her. "This feels right."

Fuck.

That was exactly how I felt too.

I covered her mouth with mine, lifting her as I had earlier. Only this time, she wrapped her legs around my waist. Her silver dress shifted up her thighs, exposing her powerful legs. I hefted her up by the ass and carried the pixie over to my bed.

"There's something I need to do," I told her through a series of kisses.

"Keep kissing me."

I obliged with a laugh. "Was planning to."

She drew my bottom lip into her mouth and bit down gently. "Where?"

I slipped a hand between our bodies. My cock was already hard as a rock to have her here, to have her want me so blatantly. But that wasn't what I was reaching for. I pressed up to what I thought would be her underwear, but I was shocked to find only bare skin.

I jerked back slightly in surprise. "You're not wearing any underwear."

Her smirk was purely devilish. "I know. It was a bad idea with all the sand. Didn't you wonder why I kept adjusting my dress?"

My mind certainly hadn't come to this conclusion. "I thought you were uncomfortable with how short it was."

"Yeah, because I wasn't ready to flash my pussy to everyone who walked by."

My cock jumped at that word out of her mouth. She must have felt it because she ground her hips in semicircles.

"I like the idea of you with no underwear on, flashing your pussy at *me*."

She dropped her legs then and set herself on her own two feet. Then, she leaned back against the bed, shifted her dress, and spread her legs. "Like this?"

"*Just* like that."

I admired the silky folds of her body as she slipped a hand down her stomach to the bead at the apex of her legs. She circled her clit a few times and then crooked a finger at me. "You said you wanted to kiss me."

Kiss had been the wrong word. I wanted to devour her.

I attacked her eagerly at the request. My tongue replaced her finger. My thumbs spread those pussy lips open, baring her entirely to me. Her head dropped backward with a moan.

"Yes," she whispered.

I brought one finger to her opening and slid it inside of her. She shuddered at the feel of me pushing in and out of her body.

"Are you imagining my cock?"

"Yes," she gasped.

A second finger followed, spreading her further. I curled my fingers inward.

"*Oh*," was all that left her mouth.

I did it again and again. I wanted her to be beyond primed. I wanted her to come so hard that she saw stars and was barely coherent. I wanted to learn all the secrets of her body.

My tongue continued flicking against her clit. She writhed on the bed. Panting gasps escaped her. I could sense that she was getting closer as her walls tightened around me. Her body so near that moment.

"Just ... just like that," she pleaded.

I did exactly what she'd said. Just held her legs wide and rode that pussy for all it was worth. A few seconds later, she shuddered as her walls contracted inward, and she cried out.

My eyes went up to hers as she orgasmed. And I got to fucking watch that masterpiece. The *O* of her mouth. The hot flush of her skin. The arch of her back. When she finally settled, I withdrew my fingers but licked her sensitive clit one more time.

She gasped and jerked away, as if even that little contact was too much.

"Holy fuck."

13

WHITLEY

Those were the only two words to describe the moment.

Gavin had made me come a week ago. It had been incredible, but he hadn't used his tongue like that. Frankly, I hadn't been aware men knew how to do that as well as women. I typically had to train them up.

But Gavin ...

He needed zero lessons.

He played my body like a violin. And I was just as vocal.

I flopped backward on the bed as he withdrew fully from my body. "Guess I should go commando more often."

He laughed. His eyes crinkled. "We could have so much fun."

That was as close as we'd come to talking about the

future. I was living in the moment. Doing exactly as he'd asked, I decided what *I* wanted. And though I probably shouldn't, what I wanted was Gavin King.

"My turn?" I asked.

"Too impatient."

He was already stripping out of his linen button-up and discarding his shorts. A bulge was evident in his boxers. My mouth watered.

"You can't be too impatient for a blow job."

"I can be when your pussy is spread open and glistening with your last orgasm."

My body heated. "Well, when you put it like that."

"Exactly."

He grabbed a condom, but I reached for it.

He shot me a questioning look as I ripped open the wrapper. I removed his boxers and took the full length of him in my hand. I jerked him up and down. A bead of pre-come lingered on the tip. I bent down and licked it off of him. It was his turn to groan. I could have worked him like an instrument too. But I could tell he wanted to be inside of me. I wanted that too.

I fitted the condom to the tip of his cock, and with practiced slowness, I drew it down over the head of him. I shot him a look that said I knew it was pure torture before dragging it down his long shaft.

"Fuck, Whit."

He spun us around. I nearly stumbled with how

quick the change was. Then, he was seated on the end
of the bed. His cock jutted upward, long and inviting.

"Come here."

I bit my lip and crawled into his lap. I tightened my
thighs to hold myself above him, not quite touching
what I wanted. He reached between us and took his
cock in his hand. Then, he slid the head back and forth
over my pussy and through the wetness. It was delicious and made me sink lower on him. He aligned our
bodies, the head slipping in with no resistance.

His hands came to my hips, and inch by glorious
inch, he eased me all the way on him. This position
was tighter and fuller. The pressure was almost too
much. Almost, but not quite painful. I was definitely
warmed up enough for him, but, dear god, it was a lot
in the best way.

"Wow," I groaned. "So ... full."

"That's right," he said as he lifted me and plunged
me hard back down on him. "Full of my cock."

I drew his lips to mine and kissed him as he worked
my hips back and forth. Every movement made me
squirm. And yet, I loved it. Wanted all of it.

"God, you feel amazing."

He tipped my head backward, moving my hands to
his knees. This position was even deeper. Shit, I could
feel him practically in my stomach.

"Oh god, Gavin."

He pushed upward into me. It was short thrusts

that I matched as best as I could, dropping onto him as he moved inside me. I hadn't thought I was close at all, but suddenly, it crept up on me like a tidal wave—growing to great heights just before it crested.

"Close," I forced out.

"Not yet," he told me.

Then, he hoisted me in his arms and pushed my back into the comfort of the mattress in one swift motion. I cried out as we reconnected in a hard thrust.

"I can't hold on."

He was pumping into me relentlessly now. "Together."

I shivered at the word as I wrapped my legs around his waist and lay there, trying everything I could to hold off until he was there too. My tidal wave broke and descended without notice.

I screamed into the villa. An entirely uninhibited sound as he shattered me whole. Then, he came down the wave with me, bursting at the seams. His head fell to my shoulder. We were sticky with sweat. Our bodies pressed tight. The climax still holding us in its clutches.

Eventually, we spun out of the spiral. My body relaxed, and I stroked up and down his back. He kissed down my shoulder, across to my neck, and down to my breasts. He licked one nipple and then the other. He bit it gently, and I jumped.

"Sensitive," I said with a laugh.

"I like it."

"Yeah, that's not the only thing you like."

He smirked, nipping at the nipple again. "No, it's certainly not."

He kissed me once and then padded into the bathroom. When he was done, I cleaned up and then returned to him. We snuggled, naked, under the covers.

The rest of the world disappeared. Everything else would return tomorrow, but tonight, we had this.

"Whit," Gavin said softly as he kissed lazily down the middle of my spine.

We'd just finished round two. Sleep beckoned, but somehow, I was still turned on. I couldn't seem to get enough of him.

"Hmm?"

"What happens when we get home?"

"What do you want to happen?"

He kissed the base of my spine. "Can't lie and say I don't want more of this. The sex is ..."

"I know," I agreed.

He hesitated, as if he had more to say.

"What?"

"Feels right, you know?"

And strangely, I did. I didn't know what to make of

these feelings. Was it just a result of the incredible sex? Gavin and I had been friends a long time. I'd always found him attractive. I'd wondered what the sex would be like. How could I not with a friend this hot? But we'd never crossed that line. I wasn't sure where that left us.

"I do," I whispered. "It does."

"Neither of us is particularly known for relationships."

I laughed softly. "Understatement."

"That doesn't mean it wouldn't work."

I rolled over to meet his green gaze. It was guarded, as if he'd said too much, made himself too vulnerable. I knew that feeling so well. My series of bad relationships was a prior that explained the future. It was why I skipped out as soon as I saw the first sign of it getting difficult. Of *me* being difficult, as always. But Gavin didn't see me that way. He never had. Even when we were only friends.

I bit my lip and nodded. "It works here."

"I thought so too." He slid up the bed to lie beside me. "Maybe we could make it work out there, in the real world. Not just here, in this secret bed. If you're willing."

Butterflies fluttered through my stomach. A feeling I hadn't had in a good long while. Oh god, I was falling for this handsome man. Falling hard. I could already

tell. And as terrifying as that revelation v
also ... exciting.

"I'm willing."

"Come here, pixie," he said with a smile as he kissed me again.

I didn't know exactly what the future held, but it looked bright. And that was enough for now.

TO BE CONTINUED

Thank you so much for reading CRUEL KISS! I adored writing this look into Gavin and Whitley's story. I've been waiting for them forever.

And I'm excited to get to write *more* of Gavin & Whit in...

A sexy stand alone fake relationship romance featuring Gavin and Whitley set in the glitz and glamour of the Cruel world from USA Today bestselling author K.A. Linde.

Turn the page to read a sneak peek at the start of the Cruel world...

CRUEL MONEY
CHAPTER 1—NATALIE

Dear Natalie,

Here are the latest rejection letters from publishers regarding TOLD YOU SO. I will follow up with a list from Caroline of the remaining publishers who have the manuscript out on submission.

Regards,

Meredith Mayberry
    Assistant to Caroline Liebermann
    Whitten, Jones, & Liebermann Literary

Enclosed:

From Hartfield:
    TOLD YOU SO has an interesting take on the

value and cost of friendship. I enjoyed the journey the characters take and style of prose. But, unfortunately, that's where my praise ends. The heroine, Karla, was a caricature of bad judgment and a complete Mary Sue in every other regard. She's plain, ordinary, and not at all interesting enough to follow for 100k words. I felt Tina might have been a better lead, but it wasn't clear from the start whether the author was knowledgeable enough to convey the true depth of either of the characters. Perhaps the author should find a muse.

From Warren:

Natalie definitely knows how to tell a story and pull the reader in with a clever introduction. I just didn't find the characters relatable or the story high concept enough for what Warren is looking for right now. For us, we weren't completely sold on the genre, as it straddles the line between women's fiction and literary and thus, sits with neither.

From Strider:

TOLD YOU SO could have been great. Karla and Tina have so much potential, and the concept, while like several things we already have in our catalog, could have been brilliant. However, I never believed in their friendship, and the middle fell flat. The pace was slow, and for once, I was actually wishing there were a romance to break up the monotony. Maybe a more talented writer could have pulled this off.

"F uck," I groaned. "I get the message."

I threw my phone on the cushion next to me. No need to torture myself by reading any more of *that*. I couldn't even believe my agent would send me those comments. Let alone on a Friday night before she left for the weekend. Even worse that it came through from her assistant with all those horrible notes about my writing.

Was this the writing on the wall? My agent was finally finding out that I was a hack. Two books and two years later with no offers and pile after pile of heartbreaking rejections. Maybe this was the end.

I stared around the beautiful Hamptons beach house I was vacation home–watching this fall. I'd been hired a month ago and shown up only three days prior, determined to finish my next manuscript. It was a dream come true to be here without any distractions— no parents or guys or anything. Just me and my computer screen.

Then, my agent had gone and dropped the biggest distraction imaginable on my plate. I glared at my screen.

Oh, hell no.

Hell. No.

I was not letting these letters set me back. Maybe

TOLD YOU SO wasn't *the* book, but the next one might be.

No, I needed to cleanse myself of this bullshit. I didn't normally subscribe to my mother's New Age spiritualism. She spent her spare time reading about auras, staring into crystal balls, and divining from the stars. It was a running joke in my life at this point. But there was a time and place for everything. And, if I was going to get something done during the next couple of months, I needed to leave the past behind me.

I knew what I was going to do.

I was going to burn this motherfucker to the ground.

Okay, maybe a little dramatic. Even for me.

But, hey, this was on the publishers. Was it so hard to craft a kind rejection email?

It's not you; it's me.

Maybe we can just be friends.

Come on. I'd heard it all from guys. Publishers could have the decency to try not to break my heart.

Ugh, fucking rejection.

But a plan had already formed, and I wasn't going to back down now.

I set my laptop up next to the printer in the office library with a bay window overlooking the ocean. I'd planned to write at that window nook. And I still wanted to. I pressed print on the computer and left to raid the stocked Kensington family wet bar. I'd have to replace whatever I scavenged, but it felt worth it tonight.

I was only watching the house through the fall season. I'd gotten the job after watching my best friend's parents' flat in Paris last summer. Word of mouth moved me around the world from there. From Paris to Turks and Caicos to Aspen, and now, I was watching the mayor of New York City's summer home in the Hamptons. And the mayor had a damn good selection of alcohol.

"Jefferson's Ocean: Aged at Sea," I muttered to myself.

Good enough for me. I grabbed the bottle and went in search of everything else I needed.

Fifteen minutes later, I had the stack of papers, a packet of matches, and the bottle of bourbon. I hoisted a shovel onto one shoulder on my way out the back door. When I hit the sand, I kicked off my shoes, grabbed a fistful of my flowy dress, and traipsed across the beach. My eyes were cast forward, and I moved with a sense of determination. The sun had finally left the horizon, throwing me into darkness, which was good, considering I was about to commit arson.

When I reached the soft sand right before the waterline, I dropped my supplies and dug my shovel into the sand. The first shovelful was incredibly satisfying. I took out my frustration and aggravation on that hole. Driving into the sand like I could erase the words from my brain. The tension in my shoulders intensified as I dug until I hit the wet sand beneath, and then I tossed my shovel to the side.

I reached for the supplies, and with my foot on the pages so that they didn't blow away, I unscrewed the top of the bottle of bourbon and took a large mouthful. The liquid burned its way down my throat. I sputtered and then took another.

That made me feel steadier. More alive. I shuddered as the alcohol hit me and then put it aside before retrieving the most important part of all of this.

Pages and pages and pages.

Forty-seven pages to be exact.

Forty-seven perfectly polite, perfectly soul-crushing pages.

Every rejection letter I'd ever gotten in the last two years, including the latest batch my agent had just sent over.

My eyes skimmed over the first page before I balled it up and threw it into the pit. A smile stretched on my face as I tossed page after page after page in the sand. Forty-seven pages of kindling.

I grinned wickedly, ready to put all of this rejection behind me.

I snatched up the bottle of bourbon and liberally poured it on the pages, like adding milk to cereal. Careful to move the bottle far enough away so that it wouldn't blow up in my face, I snatched up the box of matches.

"This is for you," I called up to the moon. "My ritual burning, my offering of this energy. Just take it away and help me start over."

I struck the match against the box and dropped it into the pit. When the first spark touched the fuel, the papers burst into flames, sending a jet of flames up toward the heavens. I laughed and danced in a circle around the flames, already feeling lighter.

So, maybe this book wasn't the one. Maybe this hadn't changed the world. But maybe the next one...or the next one. And, even if it was none of them, I was a writer. I would never stop writing.

A weight dropped off my shoulders, and I tilted my head back toward the moon. I flung my hands out to the sides and did a poorly executed turn, tripped over my own feet, and landed in a heap in the sand. But nothing could stop the euphoria that settled in my chest. Who knew it would be so liberating to burn my rejection letters?

All I'd wanted was to change my luck and let the past go, but damn I felt like a million bucks.

The flames grew and grew, burning through the last two years of my life. And I rode the high as power threaded through me, leaving me drunk and not just from the bourbon.

Jumping back to my feet, I didn't even bother

glancing down the beach. No one was in the Hamptons during the off-season. That was why I'd been hired to take care of the place during the interior renovation. Just last weekend, wealthy children of wealthy businessmen and wealthy politicians and wealthy celebrities had flocked to these beaches and overrun them at all hours of the day. But tonight, I was safe.

I wrenched at the bottom of my dress and lifted all the many layers of flowy material over my head. Tossing it into the sand, I unclasped my bra and discarded it as well. Then with a cry of triumph, I walked with my head held high straight into the ocean. The water was a bit frigid, and I shivered against the first wave that broke against my naked body. But I didn't care. I wasn't here for a swim. I was here for primal cleansing. Burn the negative energy and wash away the last remnants.

I dunked my head under the water and laughed when I breached the surface. This was what it was to live. This was what I needed to remember. Life went on.

The Kensington house was just another job. Just another way to make a living while I pursued my passion. One day, I would catch a break, but until then, I would be damned if I let those publishers bring me down. I'd put one foot in front of the other and make it work.

Confident that the ritual burning and impromptu

skinny-dipping had done its job, I hurried back out of the water. My steps were light as air, and my smile was magnetic. Whatever spell my mother's crazy life-journey had cast over all of this nonsense, it sure seemed to work. Believe in anything enough, and belief would turn into reality.

But as I was tramping back up to the fire to collect my clothes, I realized with horror that I wasn't alone. And what was worse, I recognized the man standing there.

I never forgot a face. And definitely not *that* face. Or the built body. Or the confident stance.

No, even though six years had passed, I would never forget Penn.

Or what he'd done to me.

ABOUT THE AUTHOR

 K.A. Linde is the *USA Today* bestselling author of more than thirty novels. She has a Masters degree in political science from the University of Georgia, was the head campaign worker for the 2012 presidential campaign at the University of North Carolina at Chapel Hill, and served as the head coach of the Duke University dance team.

She loves reading fantasy novels, binge-watching Supernatural, traveling to far off destinations, baking insane desserts, and dancing in her spare time.

She currently lives in Lubbock, Texas, with her husband and two super-adorable puppies.

Visit her online: www.kalinde.com
Or Facebook, Instagram & Tiktok: @authorkalinde
For exclusive content, free books, and giveaways every month. www.kalinde.com/subscribe